Elizabeth Loredo

Boogie Bones

illustrated by Kevin Hawkes

G. P. Putnam's Sons • New York

The first has always been for Julie Ann,
and for the joy that came after—Jessica
—EL

To Jon and Linda, who can dance
—KH

Text copyright © 1997 by Elizabeth Loredo. Illustrations copyright © 1997 by Kevin Hawkes
All rights reserved. This book, or parts thereof, may not be reproduced in any form without permission
in writing from the publisher. G. P. Putnam's Sons, a division of The Putnam & Grosset Group,
200 Madison Avenue, New York, NY 10016. G. P. Putnam's Sons, Reg. U.S. Pat. & Tm. Off.
Published simultaneously in Canada. Printed in Hong Kong by South China Printing Co. (1988) Ltd.
Text set in Worcester Round. Book design by Gunta Alexander.
Library of Congress Cataloging-in-Publication Data
Loredo, Elizabeth. Boogie Bones / Elizabeth Loredo; illustrated by Kevin Hawkes. p. cm.
Summary: Boogie Bones, a skeleton who loves to dance, disguises himself as a living person and leaves
his graveyard home to enter a dance contest. [1. Dancing—Fiction. 2. Skeleton—Fiction. 3. Contests—
Fiction.] I. Hawkes, Kevin, ill. II. Title. PZ7.L8787Bo 1996 [E]—dc20 95–42573 CIP AC
ISBN 0-399-22763-6 10 9 8 7 6 5 4 3 2 1 First Impression

Boogie Bones loved to dance.

There was nothing he liked more than shaking a leg, cutting a rug, or tripping the light fantastic.

He liked to dance under the cold, white spotlight of the moon, to the music of the wind shushing through the dry leaves and the tick-tick sound of the other skeletons snapping their bony fingers.

No one in Mount Stilly could match him.

But Boogie Bones longed for the chance to really show his stuff, in the world beyond the graveyard's iron gates,

Then one night a whirring wind blew a hat into the graveyard. Tucked inside was a flyer that read: DANCE CONTEST SATURDAY! COME ONE, COME ALL, TO THE TOWN HALL. PRIZES! MUSIC! ROMANCE!

That was the night Boogie Bones hatched his daring plan.

No other skeleton had ever left the graveyard, except to go trick-or-treating on Halloween night. They were all just a bit frightened of people, who had no bones about them. Even Boogie's teeth chattered a little at the thought.

But the evening of the contest, the wind whistled a haunting waltz that made the treetops bow and dance. It seemed a night for bold deeds.

And when Boogie told the other skeletons his scheme, they thought it was a grand idea. They lent him a moldy old tuxedo and some fine black patent leather shoes. He used the hat to hide his shiny white head.

When Boogie Bones was all dressed up, you could hardly tell he was a skeleton at all.

Hardly.

Boogie left the graveyard and danced off along the road in the moonlight, his shadow as a partner. But when the great iron gates disappeared from view, his courage slipped away. As he got farther and farther from the comfort of the graveyard, his steps grew slower and slower.

By the time he reached the town hall, Boogie's teeth were chattering. Only the sounds of fiddles shivering and a piano plunking made him open the big wooden door.

The town hall was crowded that night with all the best dancers in the county. Even some of the worst. The judge was a tall, thin man who once had ridden in an elevator with the great dancer Fred Astaire.

When Boogie Bones got there, a cha-cha was in full swing. And right in the middle of the floor, a man and woman were dancing all alone. The man had a beard like a tumbleweed, but that wasn't what made Boogie stop and stare.

No doubt about it. These two were the county's top dancers. Boogie could feel it in his bones.

Cha Cha cha-cha-cha. Cha Cha cha-cha-cha.

Back and forth they trotted, noses turned up and toes turned down. Back and forth they rocked like a hobbyhorse on its spring. Then, with a quick twirl and a swirl of satin, the cha-cha ended.

If Boogie had had a heart, it would have sunk right down to his shiny patent leather shoes. He hadn't seen dancing so pretty since the night he watched a black widow spider do a waltz on her web. A spindleshanks had no place on a dance floor with the likes of them.

Boogie's shoulders slumped. His tuxedo sighed and settled sadly, like a flour sack, on his bones. He hid behind a potted palm and told himself he wouldn't dance at all that night.

That's when the opening notes of a tango filled the air.
A tango!

Boogie Bones swayed.

He tapped his toes. He twitched his hips. Before he knew what he was doing, Boogie Bones was dancing in the corner, with the palm as his partner. The green leaves rustled and shook, but no one noticed.

Well, almost no one.

But when the tango music reached its peak, Boogie couldn't hide his light behind a palm tree any longer. He didn't care about being the best. He had to dance.

Boogie burst from his corner and grabbed a partner from the line of ladies by the wall. Together they tangoed across the room.

"What a wonderful dancer," the crowd murmured.

"He tangos better than Fred Astaire," said the tall, thin judge to himself. "But of course, there wasn't a lot of room in that elevator."

Boogie Bones's partner thought she was the luckiest woman alive.

When the music stopped, the whole crowd applauded. They begged Boogie Bones to dance again.

He and his partner did a mambo. They rumba-ed and they waltzed. The bearded dancer grew so jealous, he dropped his partner in mid-dip and flounced off the dance floor in a rage.

Still, everything would have been fine. But then the band began to play "Jumpin' at the Woodside." It was Boogie Bones's favorite tune.

He started to lindy hop.

Boogie Bones's feet flew faster than a flock of crows. He wriggled and he jiggled back and forth across the dance floor while the crowd clapped and cheered . . .

until his hat flew off.

And he wiggled right out of his tuxedo.

An eerie sound filled the room.

Oooooooooooooo.

Someone screamed. The tall, thin judge fainted dead away. The band stopped playing.

Boogie Bones's partner muttered "It figures," as she crept back to her seat against the wall.

It looked like winning the dance contest was out of the question.

Then a little girl stood up on her chair in the corner. Her name was Maggie Brown. She wore Boogie Bones's hat tilted at a rakish angle over her braided hair. She said, "I'm not afraid of any old bones!"

And she climbed down off her chair and held out her hand to Boogie Bones.

He bowed.
She curtsied.
(They taught it in school.)
They started to dance.

The crowd stood quaking in their boots. The noise of their knees knocking and teeth rattling sounded like music to Boogie Bones. He spun Maggie around and around until her braids were a blur and her skirt spread like a blossom.

After a while the people watching began to feel a little silly. There they stood, hair on end like a row of dried cornstalks, while little Maggie Brown danced the lindy hop, not the least bit scared. It just didn't seem right.

So one by one they began to clap.

The band leader shrugged his shoulders and lifted his baton. The band went right back to playing "Jumpin' at the Woodside" while Boogie Bones and Maggie danced and danced.

It was the best lindy hop that crowd had ever seen.

Even the judge, when he revived, had to agree.

That was the happiest night of Boogie Bones's life.